THE CHRONICLES OF GREAT BRITAIN'S FIRST EVER VAMPIRE TEDDY BEAR

by Christopher Plumridge

SPECIAL NOTE

SPECIAL NOTE ON SONGS AND RECORDINGS

Cover Art Design: Martha Lysa
Book Design: Jonathan Cook
First Edition: August 2024
ISBN 978-1-964045-05-4

Dedicated to my wife Jackie, the ever-present light in my life.

Special thanks to Martha Lysa for her beautiful art, to Alex Goodchild for her unwavering support for all my written work and to the many wonderful playwrights I've met from around the world for their guidance, valuable critique and love.

THE BEAR: BEGINNINGS by Christopher Plumridge first premiered as an animated short film produced by RubySky Productions. Directed and edited by Christopher Plumridge with artwork by Martha Lysa. The cast was as follows:

BEAR . . . . Dale Wylde

The film was a finalist at:
Short + Sweet (2023)

And was screened at:
The MMM New Jersey (2024)
Imagina AniFest New York (2023)
TMFF Festival Glasgow (2023)
   **Audience Favourite Award*

THE CHRONICLES OF GREAT BRITAIN'S FIRST EVER VAMPIRE TEDDY BEAR

CHARACTERS

THE BEAR
Male – Plot Specific. Any age and race. Should have a posh, well spoken, English accent.

VOICE (optional)
Child(ren) – To voice an English boy and a German girl.

HEATHER (optional)
Female - Plot specific. Any age and race. Ideally a British accent.

PLACE
Various locations.

TIME
Various times in history and the present, where specified.

AUTHOR NOTES

The Bear monologues contained within can either be performed all together for an evening of theater or may be performed individually as needed.

The character, The Bear, should have an air of self-importance, without being rude or condescending. Take time to read his words and understand his voice. Have fun with him and enjoy the ride.

The setting can be as simple as an empty stage, or as realized as the producer desires.

<u>PART 1 - BEGINNINGS</u>

In this opening episode, we witness the creation of The Bear as he is being prepared for his future child owner, but this is 1940s Frankfurt, and all is not so calm in the world...

BEAR: This is the story of my humble beginnings, you will find out later how I became Great Britain's first ever Vampire Teddy Bear. For now, let me take you back, far back to 1941 Frankfurt. Twas a dark and stormy night . . .

. . . but not like any other, for yet again, this was no natural storm, no heaven-sent storm from above. No, this storm came from those hideous big metal bats from the skies, dropping their pain and destruction on our otherwise peaceful city! My maker, Franz, had barely finished me when his whole house and his whole world shook. He said to me in his minty breath, (His breath was always fresh from the peppermints he sucked, I believe they helped him concentrate.) "Ah, you are fine bear! You will make a child very happy indeed." With that he tied my red silk bow round my neck and gave me a tickle under my chin. I looked up in wonderment to his beaming smile shining through his scruffy grey beard, a sight that will stay with me for the rest of my days. Moments later, Franz's front door received a heavy, desperate, urgent knocking! Franz grabbed me, tucked me inside his big fur lined coat, I teddy plunged into darkness, but I could certainly hear what was happening. Held tight under his arm, away from harm he rushed downstairs to answer the door, but it was too late, for before him I could hear the door being ripped from its hinges, wood splintered around my ears! There came a voice, booming, bellowing and angry! "CHEW!" As my maker stepped back in protest, I could not understand what the big gruesome voice meant by CHEW, surely Franz only sucked on peppermints? We were dragged out of the house, I clung onto the inside of my makers coat for dear life, as we were flung into one of those infernal, noisy motorized carriages. We were pushed into the corner of this terrible smoky machine, as it sped away, throwing us here, chucking us there, I could hear Franz shouting his distaste. But within a few moments he went quiet for he must have been struck, a small trickle of blood ran down his chest beside me. Although I could feel the comforting hand of my maker around me through his coat, I dared not breathe a breath for the remaining journey. Then all of a terrible sudden the motorized monster stopped and we were dragged clear to lots of shouting, abuse and confusion! As Franz was being forced to walk along, his coat blew open slightly so I could see were now in a frantic place of steam and screams called Frankfurt Bahnhof. Maker! Please take me back to your house, it is calm there, with the other Bears, I do not like this place! But there was no way back, no way could my maker help us now, we were thrown onto a big, long, metal snake that spat dirty grey smoke into the dark and sorry sky. All around I could hear people crying, I caught glimpses of other bears like me, held in the innocent hands of frightened little children. Then I heard Franz say, "There's no need to be scared, what is your name young lady?" To which a quiet, quivering voice replied "Hilda." My master kneeled down, took me from his coat and placed me in the arms of this child before him, then he whispered, "Hilda, take this bear, he will protect you. See that gap in the door? Take the bear and run through it, run away from this train, run as fast as your little legs will take you, run for as long as you can bear and never look back!"

We were off! Hilda holding me upside down by my foot as she ran and ran, bless her she could run fast! She ran just as my maker had instructed, never looking back, never hesitating, as shouts and bullets flew past our ears! In time, she grew tired, but still she jogged, holding me tight, close against her chest so I could feel her tears dripping on my dirty, disheveled fur. Poor Hilda was close to giving up, close to collapsing there in the road when we were both swept up into the air and I was thrown clear into the mud! Face down I could hear Hilda cry out "Bear!" and seconds later I could feel a big firm hand grab me, nigh on taking the wind out of me and I was thrown into a motorized car alongside Hilda, reunited! A deep male voice spoke out in a strange language, over the rattily old engine as we were sped away, "Viens avec nous, tu es en sécurité maintenant!"

Days later Hilda and I found ourselves in a little wooden cabin on a mountainside, a log fire flicked its gentle light dance around us as Hilda and I sat on a lovely, deep, soft rug. Hilda was now wearing a pretty dress, her golden hair all curly and for the first time I saw her laugh! My fur was now clean and fluffy, my red bow re-tied and my only sadness was the memory of my maker, wondering when he would join us in our heavenly hillside hideaway. Hilda sometimes held me up by the window so we could see over the snow-covered mountains, but my biggest memory of that wooden cabin was the blasted clock! You would hardly believe me when the damn thing spat out a crazy little bird with its lunatic call, Cuckoo! Cuckoo! Every single hour!

EVERY SINGLE HOUR, day and night! I will get that blasted little bird if it's the last thing I do!

(Blackout.)

<u>PART 2 - CRIB OF DOOM</u>

Our Bear is caught in a difficult predicament. He is trapped in a child's crib. The morning sun is casting its beam across the bed of the crib. Being a Vampire, this could end him. . .

BEAR: Let me get this straight from the start, alike a hero of mine Yogi, I am NOT your average bear. Yes, I am a small brown stuffed toy bear - the type you see most babies and young children cuddle, play with, force imaginary cups of tea into, swing upside down by one foot and generally abuse on a daily basis. But there is a darker side to me. I am also a Vampire Bear. Don't ask me how this came about, that is a story for later, I simply haven't the time to go into this given my current predicament. You see I am currently trapped in this high walled wooden slatted prison chamber the humans call a cot. Even a vampire bear such as myself cannot escape (I wasn't blessed with the whole 'turn into a bat' power). But that is the least of my worries right now. The morning sun has been for the last hour rolling across the room on its unstoppable path towards me. As I am a vampire bear, I cannot be exposed to direct sunlight, it would spell Hell for me with a capital 'H'. If I had the bones and muscles you humans take for granted, I could push myself away from the sun beam, even climb out of this soft bedded jail, but no, I am just a humble stuffed vampire bear remember! How can these humans of mine leave me here alone to face a long painful burning death after all I have done for them? I never even tried to bite the baby, despite its milky white soft skin through which I could almost smell the blood pumping through the jugular. I have taken all the regular mishandling as already mentioned above with dignity and pose but for all this they still neglect me! Why? Oh no! The sun light is getting closer now, I can feel the heat warming my left foot! I start trying to flap my arms in the vain attempt to fly, hoping beyond all hope that somehow I did inherit the turning into a bat thing. But I am stuck, the only things running is my frantic mind and the shaft of light promising to perish me alive! I probably have only a minute left, where are they? Can't the baby help me now? I don't care if I end up face down in some disgusting porridge just save me! Just when I think all is lost and I'm about to watch my foot burst into flames I feel a pressure around my stomach. Yes! A big human hand has grabbed me, lifting me out of my crib coffin and flying me to safety. Boy that was close. Ha! All in a day's work for a vampire bear like me! Now let me tell you about the day I became the Great Britain's first ever Vampire Teddy Bear. It was a dark and stormy night . . .

(Blackout.)

<u>PART 3 - REBORN</u>

Here The Bear explains his transformation, in true gothic style, from a humble stuffed bear to a Vampire Teddy Bear.

BEAR: Let me tell you how I became Great Britain's first ever Vampire Teddy Bear. Twas a dark and stormy night, yes I appreciate that is a tad cliche, but it really was, so kindly bear with me. Ahem. Twas a dark and stormy night, I lay huddled in bed with Baby Jonathan in the third-floor bedroom of Castle Dracula, Transylvania, home to Cousin Steiff. I joined the family in what they call a vacation, a place to go to 'clear their heads', a concept I will never understand, surely their heads are full of stuffing like mine? One night, all around the castle the clouds rumbled their heavy distaste and threw down great bolts of electricity which lit up the cold stone walls and sent flickers of frightening shadows dancing round our bed. My fur stood on end and although Baby Jonathan was of no real protection to a simple stuffed bear such as myself, I found myself edging closer to him. Instinctively he put a soft fleshy smooth arm around me and for once in my life I am happy to admit I enjoyed his slobbery kiss on my fur. I had a fitful sleep, as soon as I drifted, another flash and rumble would startle us. Baby cried, I shivered, the bed shook. Then all of a terrible sudden the window blew open, the curtains reared up towards us, the wind whipped around our old cold room. That's when I first saw her, first set my old bear eyes on her staggering beauty. I had been told of stories of old of her legend, but nothing could prepare me for the sight I saw before me. Cousin Steiff stood tall and proud on the window ledge, laughing manically, the wind whipping up her black cloak around her slender shoulders, the window slammed shut behind her and within a second she stood at my feet! How? I looked up in abject fear, bearly believing the vision before me. I had heard Cousin Steiff was beautiful, but her beauty held me still and captivated me! Her Mohair fur so soft and sleek, (my heart bleeds for the poor Mo animal that gave up its hide!) her eyes so crystal clear you could see your own impending doom within them! Her gold stitching, my word so neat, so precise! This was a beautifully crafted bear if ever there was, she lured me in with a smile and I was powerless to her charms. I looked to Baby Jonathan for support, but he was sound asleep, thumb in mouth, his blond hair in a curl on his forehead. As I looked back to the stunning Steiff, her crystal eyes glowed a fiery yellow, she bucked her head back to reveal two grotesque, long white fangs glowing in a flash of lightning! I had no time to move, no breath to scream, no fight in my limbs when Cousin Steiff bore down on me, those big white teeth sunk into my neck! I was paralysed, disgusted, but I lusted for this exquisite bear! I wanted to kiss her, wrap her in my arms, feel her silky fur in my paws but she was gone! The night was now calm, the moon shone delicate beams across the bedroom floor and a subtle cool breeze blanketed me. But inside I felt more alive than ever, she had literally knocked the stuffing out of me and replaced it with the same fire, heat and passion as those electric bolts the clouds rained down upon us the previous eve!

There followed a hideous journey home, by rickety old cart pulled by angry snarling horses, me upside down, stuffed tight in an old leather holdall, having to endure a hideously sickening crossing over the North Sea before finally docking in Whitby Harbour at one a.m. There I was finally released from my baggage entrapment and allowed to travel with Baby Jonathon in the back of the family motorised car. Never before have I felt so alive, so much passion, so much hunger for blood and fur . . . I had been . . . REBORN!

(Blackout.)

<u>PART 4 - BEAR TAKES MANHATTAN</u>

Bear, whilst on a city break to New York, finds himself alone in a top floor suite of a famous hotel. He is by the window looking down on Manhattan, planning his take-over of New York . . .

BEAR: This is the story of how I, Great Britain's first ever Vampire Bear took Manhattan and the whole of New York! Twas a bright and stormless night . . .

"Humans and Teddy Bears of Manhattan, listen to me and listen well, for I am Great Britain's first ever Vampire Bear and I come to you from the Empire suite atop of the Four Seasons Hotel! Yes, be afraid, be very afraid, stop in the streets and stare in wonder at your nearest televisual device. For I have already taken over the broadcasting stations of Manhattan, New York and Beyond! See me on your screens in the Bars of Brooklyn, The Sidewalks of Staten Island, The Malls of Manhattan, The Backstreets of the Bronx, The Lobbies of Long Island and the Qu . . . the Qu . . . the . . . oh curse my stuffing brain . . . erm . . . everywhere in Queens! I am in your EYES! I am in your EARS! I am in your MINDS! Bow beneath me and beg for your lives, cover your necks and beg for mercy, drop to your knees and beg for your souls! Do not send in your police humans with their batons and bullets, for I am in-turmoil, I mean IMMORTAL! Leave your crosses in your churches, they do not offend me. Leave your garlic in your grocery stores, their smell does not bother me. Leave your silver bullets . . . actually yes, just leave them please! Leave your . . ."

(Beep beep sound effect.)

'What's this? Who dares interrupt me when I've barely got going? How very bear you? A text message? *(reads)* 'Riddle me here, riddle me there, who's afraid of a little . . . brown . . . bear . . ?' What is this insolence, who text this tripe? Do you not realise who I am? One more message like that and you'll find yourself slumped in the corner of the elevator of the Four Seasons Hotel, like Boris the bolshy bellhop with two blood dripping holes from his neck! Boy, the boy tasted good, rejuvenating! Ha!'

'Where was I? Ah yes, taking Manhattan!'

"Humans and Teddys, lurk in the alleys, quiver in the shadows, hide behind the dumpsters, Etcetera . . . Etcetera, for tonight I will walk amongst you! I have a hunger, a yearning, a lust for blood and fur, my needs you will incur! I like that, it rhymes!"

(Distracted by something in the sky.)

'What on earth now? Ha! Do you think shining a 'bat wing signal' into the night sky will do you any good? Your bat man is long gone, he can't save you now, this isn't Gotham you know!'

"Bow to me, the Vampire Bear, bring me your children and their Teddy Bears, sacrifice them to save yourselves! Feed me their blood and fur, flesh and stuffing, their soft skin necks and stitching! You may see me as just another Bear full of cotton stuffing, but it's not who I am underneath, but what I do that defines me!"

'This is so much fun, if only Cousin Steiff could see me now!'

"The night is darkest just before dawn, and humans of

Manhattan, your dawn is coming! Run for your lives, cower in your swanky loft apartments, go to -

VOICE: There he is Mummy! On the window ledge looking out over the city! Hehe! Silly Ol' Bear!

(Bear is grabbed by a human hand, cuddled and dragged off stage.)

BEAR: 'Unhand me at once! Let go of me, Jonathan! Can't you see I'm busy taking Manhattan! Oh the indignity! Fine! Just don't carry me upside down please, the blood runs to my head.'

(Blackout.)

<u>PART 5 - BEAR SAVE THE QUEEN!</u>

In July 1982, intruder Michael Fagan successfully managed to break into Buckingham Palace and even made it into the Her Majesty's Bedroom where he came face to face with Queen Elizabeth II. This is The Bear's version of events that night . . .

BEAR: Let me tell you about the day I, Great Britain's first ever Vampire Bear, saved the life of our Gracious Queen, Elizabeth II. Twas not a dark and stormy night, just a tad glum and drizzly. Jonathan, his family and I, in the little mites sticky, sweaty mitts, had nearly come to the end of our grand tour of Buckingham Palace, just before having to endure the inevitable shop before the exit with its hideous little London tourist trinkets, was dropped by the aforementioned Jonathan amidst a tantrum bought on by the fact his parents would not allow him to 'do potty' in Prince Philip's commode. Oh my that was a long sentence, do try to stay with me! There I was, on the floor of the Grand Hall of Buckingham Palace, so many portraits of noble Kings and Queens looked down upon this humble Bear! Above them a huge arch of the most stunning and beautiful murals framed in sparkling gold lit up my sky! I lay in wonderment as the lights began to go out around me, all I could hear was the click clack of the warden's feet on the old flagstones as he turned off each light in turn. I was all alone. For an hour I lay, my back cold against the floor, my fir all goosebumps as the chill kicked in. Then, just as I felt my sleep overcoming me a small shaft of light slipped across the floor. This was no sunlight, thank heavens, for that would spell hell for me with a capital H, remember? This light was gentle, warm, as if from a single candle, it flicked the faces of the former monarchs. I could hear subtle soft shuffling from delicate feet until above me a kindly old lady looked down at this cold and lonely bear. She spoke in the most beautiful, eloquent tone "Oh my, what is this? Gosh, a cute little bear!" She picked me up, held me up in front of her and straightened my red bow. "Some poor child must have left you behind, I will see that a servant delivers you to the Palace lost and found department where you can be reunited with your owner." There came another voice from across the hall, "What are you up to Lilibet?" To which the gracious gentlewoman replied. "Nothing Philip, go back to sleep and do try not to snore so, it disturbs one's corgis."

She carried me into her chamber, sat me on a fine and luxurious chaise lounge, gave me another sweet smile with a twinkle in her eye and bade me goodnight little bear. She climbed up into a huge bed, with four big posts holding up a roof of the finest red velvet drapes. This was by far a far grander cot than Jonathan's crib! Soon settled I could hear her breathe softly as she slipped into a peaceful sleep. I became alarmed when I noticed across the room the window was slightly open, surely it was a wet but warm night. I decided to stand guard, keep my beady bear eye open on that window to protect this sweet old mam. But it had been a long day, hours being dragged though London on dirty tunnel trains which drew up such vicious winds to ruffle my already dirty, smokey fur! I began to grow tired, my bear eyes watched the open window until sleep finally overcame me.

Then all of a terrible sudden the window flew open to a great thunderbolt of lightning, my hairs stood on end and the curtains rippled up in the blinding flash of light. There stood a figure, there afore the very window in the darkest silhouette. Cousin Steiff? Is that you? This is no time to pay a visit now! But no, this was not Cousin Steiff, this silhouette was far taller than any bear I've met. In another huge flash of lightning this creature standing before me was revealed. Behold, just a man, a normal man of average height similar to Jonathan's father I'd say. I could hear a quiet trembling coming from the sweet old lady's bed, I looked across to see her sitting up, her satin sheets drawn up to her chin as she shook in fear! The man slowly walked towards us, a manic, angry look swept across his average face, I could not stand by, I had to protect this altruistic angel. I summoned up all my strength and resolve, stood high on my fat furry feet and leapt forward at this intrepid intruder! Flying through the air I could hear the old lady cry out "Bear!" I landed directly on the snoopers shoulder, let out my best battle cry (simply for added effect I must admit) and sank my vampire bear teeth into this ne'er-do-well's neck! He let out a dreadful scream, throwing me clear and I landed in the sweet old lady's arms! We looked towards the window, the average Joe interloper had dropped to the floor clutching his neck and sobbing like a baby! All this commotion invited swarms of guards, butlers and maids into the charming chamber. We were safe, our night stalker was dragged away as a maid settled the old lady with a glass of warm milk. All was well again as I was held in her arms, in the softest most luxurious bed I have ever snuggled in. The storm had passed, all was quiet except a subtle snoring and snorting coming from the adjoining chamber.

Days later, Jonathan, his family and I found ourselves in a spectacular hall, it's ceiling higher than the clouds themselves, angels looked down upon this bashful bear. I appeared to be the focus of all the attention, which naturally I wallowed in! Jonathan, holding me by one paw, his mother holding the other, took me to the front and I was placed on the most luxuriant red cushion. I looked up, again in wonderment, to see the gracious old lady looking at me with that sweet smile. This time she was dressed in the most beautiful garments imaginable, a glorious crown of the most glistening jewels adorned her head. But then her face grew stern as she drew up an enormous sword, high above her head! Clearly, she knew her vampire mythology, how could she want to behead me after I saved her life? Is there no compassion for a tiny timid teddy? If I could have screamed and ran, I most certainly would have! I clenched my eyes tight closed, gritted my vampire bear teeth and gripped the cushion for dear life! But she simply tapped each of my fluffy shoulders with her long blunt sword and said,

"Arise, Sir Bear!"

(Blackout.)

<u>PART 6 - EXIT, PURSUED BY A VAMPIRE BEAR!</u>

Bear accidently finds himself in the limelight after saving Shakespeare's Globe Theatre, and his family, from certain doom.

BEAR: This is the story of how I, Great Britain's first ever Vampire Teddy Bear, made my stage debut! Yes, it was a surprise to me too!

Twas a dark and stormy night in old London Town, you could barely see across the river Thames, for on this eve in question it resembled an old Turner Painting. Battered old barges belched out thick grey smog into the already gloomy sky as they plied their trade up and down the river. I was being carried by young Jonathan as we made due haste along London Bridge, just as well we sped for he and his family were singing about it falling down! Would we make it in time? Alas we did, and soon we found ourselves on the south bank of this dark, grey, forbidding river.

We stood in wonderment at a glorious great globe of a theatre, its stark white walls and sturdy oak beams adorned by a thick straw roof stood high afront us! We were soon inside, sheltering from the incessant drizzle, when the little mite insisted on taking off his coat. Earlier that day, back in the warmth of Claridge's Hotel, said little mite demanded that "If *I* have to wear a coat, so does Bear!" I was adorned with a thick black cloak, tied tightly around my neck, which once festooned, flapped freely and I dare say fantastically in the wind behind me. I relished this look! I am such stuffing as dreams are made of! Jonathan was persuaded to keep his coat and hat on, he would need them for the show and I was pleased to be cloaked, for this strange circular structure had a huge hole in the roof! Had they not the funds to fill the ceiling of this handsome hall? The family found some space not far from a raised platform which seemed to be the focus of the ever increasing throng of theatre goers. Mist turned into rain, the rain turned heavier by the minute, but still his parents remained, waiting patiently, smiles beamed across their faces in eager anticipation. Then the show began, something about a winters tail, but none of these actor fellows had tails! I was sure all would become clear as the story began to unfold. After much ado between Lords and Ladies, all harking on about a land by the name of Bohemia, Jonathan and I soon drew tired and weary. But at least it had stopped raining at last. I looked up through this airy auditorium at the angry grey clouds glaring down upon us… I heard a distant rumble… the crowds cheered . . . then . . . all of a terrible sudden . . . a great bolt of light crashed down onto the shelter of straw! But no-one saw, except for this humble Bear! I kept focus on where this lightning bolt had struck and sure enough a fire began to break out, this would make a hay hood of a disaster! I shook myself clear of Jonathan's grasp, ran through the feet of the thespian fans and entered the outer ring of this bizarre build. I ran for the wooden steps where a big brute of a man named Warwick stood in my way! To bite or not to bite, that was my question. I explained to this strapping sentinel of stairs, of the impending ill luck of the infrastructure when he just held up his hand and said . . . nothing! For I had already surged to his shoulder, bit into his ruffled neck and left him blubbering at the bottom step! Alas poor Warwick, I did not know him well.

On the third floor I perchance to notice a coiled red snake hung on the wall, a sign above read 'WATER'. I had seen Jonathan's father put out a garden bonfire with water, so I grabbed the head of this slinky serpent and tugged it up to the top of the roof where I was faced with fearsome flickers of furious flames! I squeezed the head of this bevel-nosed boa and a fast stream of water sprayed over the thatch of fire. I swung it here, swung it there, swung it everywhere! Soon the fire was out and I took in a big bear breath and relaxed. But below, in the antique amphitheatre, came calls and cheering! "Bear! Bear! Bear!" I stood tall and proud upon their horizon, my black cape flapping in the wind against distant flashes of lightning which lit up the London sky! Once again I took up the watery snake, wrapped it in my arms and swung down heroically onto the stage afront of my fascinated fans. An actor fellow by the name of Antigonus, with a babe in arms, stood in my way, taking my limelight! So I chased him off, exit pursued by a Vampire Bear haha! I stood centre stage, my public adoring me, calling out "A Bear, A Bear, our kingdom for a Bear!" I calmed down my adoring audience with a flash of my vampire fangs and addressed them: "Friends, Romans, countrymen, lend me your Bears!" to which a voice cried out above all the others, my best friend Jonathan! "Bear!" he called. I threw myself into the throng and soon found myself back in the arms of the little mite!

"Come along Bear," said Jonathan's mother, "It's time we should go."

Jonathan held me up high above his little head as I shouted out "Farewell my fellows, parting is such sweet sorrow!"

(Blackout.)

<u>PART 7 - DIAMONDS ARE FOR HEATHER</u>

During the early hours of November 7th, 2000, at the Millennium Dome, London, a gang led by William Cockram attempted the theft of the Millennium Star Diamond. Reports stated that London's Met Police thwarted their attempt. This is the Bears version of what really happened.

BEAR: This is the Story of how I, Great Britain's first ever Vampire Teddy Bear, foiled Great Britain's biggest ever Diamond Heist! Yes, do not believe the tosh you read in the tabloids, the glory was all mine!

Twas a dark and stormy night across London town, which is completely irrelevant in this story actually, for we were safely under the big, glistening white roof of the Millennium Dome. Jonathan and his family, I tucked suitably under his arm, were visiting the wonderful exhibition to commemorate the year two thousand. We spent time clamoring through some great big fellow's limbs and body, the strangest reversal to an outer body experience, I can tell you. This poor giant human must have felt quite peculiar having little people and bears coursing through his veins. We trudged round many other scientific and educational exhibits while Jonathan became tired, weary . . . and demanding ice cream. We stood in awe at the De Bears Diamond Exhibition; the Millennium Star Diamond was centerpiece, perfect and exquisite, flawless, much like myself! However, his patience finally wore out. Abated with a tub of Ben and Jerry's, we soon found ourselves deep in the center of this colossal cone, we took seats around a circular stage and waited for the big show to begin. The lights dimmed, stirring music filled our ears, a light mist rolled across the stage. Then from the center, a great orange cone of the finest silk arose, being held aloft by flying humans! Are they vampires too? Surely not! Alas, on closer inspection they seemed to be attached by fine wires suspended from the ceiling. As the show progressed, the audience marveled at the display above their heads as acrobats flew here, swung there and wrapped themselves in the fiery silk and spun like candy floss! We were very close to the front, (nothing but the best seats for Bear and Co), when one highly skilled sky dancer dropped in front of us. Wow! She was so beautiful, slim and sporty, dare I say . . . sexy? As Jonathan's mother closed the gaping jaw of Jonathan's father, this perfect performer leant down to whisper in the little mite's ear. He vehemently nodded and passed me to this lovely, luscious lady of the lines, she gave me a kiss on my head and held me up high for all the throng to see. Of course, I enjoyed the attention but not as much as her soft skinned but strong hands around me. Just as I found myself falling in love with this dashing dancer, we were swept high in the air and in seconds, she was upside down, the spotlights picking up her long flowing golden hair, eye emerald eyes sparkling, her lips so . . . ahem, where was I?! Yes! To my utter shock she threw me to another active acrobat, but your Bear had other plans, instinct kicked in and I began to fly by my own accord. I swopped here, dived there, dodged the flaying arms of all those who tried to catch me during their sensational show. All around me I could hear rapturous applause and cries of 'Bear! Bear! Bear!' As I flew, the glamourous girl called out on each passing "Where" *swing* "Did" *swing* "You" *swing* "Learn" *swing* "to" *swing* "FLY LIKE THAT?" A few moments later she had taken me backstage for a drink and recovery, where she told me her name was Heather. Naturally, I bowed gracefully, proffered my hand, did kiss hers and introduced myself as *The* Bear. "We must work on an act together, the audiences will love it even more than what they just saw!" she proclaimed.

We practiced through the night, many times I flew, many times she caught me, we were like bats in the belfry on a dark stormy night, flying only on instinct and sound. We were . . . alone. Alone in the dome. On our own, in the . . . zone . . .

Just as we had polished our outlandish offering there came, all of a terrible sudden, a great crashing through the wall! For right ahead of us a giant yellow digging machine trundled into view, the wall of this great dome splintered either side of this gnarling beast! Two masked men jumped clear of it and ran to towards the diamond exhibition. Poor Heather was terrified at the sight, so I gently whispered in her ear, she nodded, sprung into action, and in seconds we were flying through the air. Just as we had practiced in rehearsal, she threw me swiftly through the air towards the masked marauders! They shouted, I flew, Heather swung past them, kicking one to the ground. Atta Girl! I soon came under attack from a barrage of blisteringly fast nails which whistled by my ear, one passed straight though my body! Fear not, for remember I am an immortal vampire bear and, let's be honest here, full of stuffing. I took my chance and dropped down on the remaining robber, sinking my Bear fangs into his neck and watching him fall. Both of these dastardly diamond displacers rolled around the floor in pain and Heather and I shared a deserved high five. Moments later the police arrived and we explained our escapade. The police officer in charge said it was all under control and they had the rascal robbers observed for some time. Naturally, I was disgusted, this is my win, MINE! I'm the hero here! Don't you know who I am? Then the police officer explained, "We have been watching these hoodlums, the diamonds are fake, we swapped them yesterday in case they got away with it. But as a reward, you brave little bear, you may have the phony diamonds!" I thanked him and made perfectly sure my name would be written in the report, so therefore distributed to the press. He hesitated briefly until a flash of my vampire bear fangs made him decide otherwise.

As he passed me the make pretend rocks, I looked into the eyes of my beautiful assistant and simply said, "No, the Diamonds are for Heather".

> *(Lights start to fade but then with a hand guesture from Bear, they rise in full again.)*

Ha! We cannot end it like this, we need a song! Take it away Heather!!

HEATHER: *(singing)* Diamonds are for Heather

> They are all I need to please me
>
> They can stimulate and tease me
>
> Twas a dark and stormy night
>
> I've no fear that they might, convert me
>
> Vampire Teddy's are forever
>
> Hold one up and then caress it
>
> Touch it, stroke it and undress it

BEAR: Oh I say!

HEATHER: *(singing)* I can see every part

> Nothing hides in the heart to Bear me
>
> Diamonds are for Heather
>
> Sparkling 'round my little finger

Unlike men, the diamonds linger
Bear is immortal too
And worth going to your grave for…..
Teddy's are forever, for Heather, forever
Diamonds are for Heather, forever, forever

BEAR: Big finish Heather!

HEATHER: *(singing)* Just like Bear, they'll live forever and ever!

(Blackout.)

<u>PART 8 - A DOGGED TAIL</u>

While Jonathan and his family enjoy a cultural visit to Edinburgh during the fringe festival, Bear meets a curious friend, and together they stumble on a ghostly legend...

BEAR: This is the story about how I, Great Britain's first ever Vampire Teddy Bear became embroiled in a dogged tail. Yes, you've spotted the play on words there, I see you're paying attention!

Twas a dark and stormy night in the City of Edinburgh, Scots Land. Jonathan and his family were enjoying a long weekend in the rainy, gloomy city, to take in some more 'theatre'. This was becoming a habit for them, a pastime they seem to thoroughly enjoy. But for the likes of me I simply cannot understand why on earth they would want to watch one man stand alone on stage, all dressed up and gabbling on about all sorts of nonsense! But here we were, stood in the rain on afore mentioned foul weathered eve, outside another theatre waiting our turn to enter the lobby of warmth and tubs of sweet popcorn. Jonathan's parents were deep in conversation with two other humans, who both had strange accents, clearly speaking English but with a disdainful dropping of their vowels! But I digress. At the feet of this foreign couple a small black dog, with subtle streaks of grey hair, stood patiently, his ears pricked up, his tail wagging gently in the wind. It looked at me, sniffed, pricked up its ears, its eyes widened. As I looked down from the little mite's arms at this curious canine, it snarled at me, its teeth sparkled in a flash of lightning!

Ha! Two can play this game my four-legged fiend! I flashed my Vampire Bear fangs at it in return. It cocked its head in bewilderment, it furrowed its brows, its ears pricked even more than before. Then to my surprise, (but I really should have expected this, for it is not uncommon for a dog to bark,) it let out a great big barrage of barks! Jonathan jumped and I fell from his arms. Barely a second I lay face down on the ancient flagstones when I was picked up by this fluffy foxhound, I could feel its teeth holding me tight, its dog slobber dampening my fur, oh the indignity! We were off! Boy, could this ruffian run! I could hear cries behind me, "BEAR!" and "BROMPTON!" The city was bustling and busy, my abductor darted between legs and lamp posts, never stopping, never pausing for breath. All around us people cheered, fellows spat fire, rode bicycles of only one wheel, dressed like bears, one fellow even balanced a ladder on his head! This was some strange and wonderous night, but I had no time to stand and stare for I had to find my escape from this terrier's teeth. In time my carrier became tired, he slowed, he huffed and panted then finally dropped me on some grass. We were in some spooky space, a peaceful park of stone slabs pointing up at the stormy sky. I looked up at this dogged fellow, its tongue slipped out from his mouth as it caught its breath, its eyes, now softer looked down at me in puzzlement, its ears dropped down by its wizened old face. Then to my utter amazement it spoke, in English! "I say, sorry about that old chap, I don't know what came over me!" to which I replied, naturally, "Oh my word a talking dog!" for which it in return replied, "Oh my word a talking teddy bear!" I exclaimed to it my distaste at being abducted and was about to sink my bear fangs into his collared nape when he released a gentle, high-pitched whine and held up a paw. Usually I am a tough, vindictive, vampire bear but something about this fluffy fellow's innocence fluttered in my heart. I introduced myself, "Good morrow fair fellow, I am *The* Bear, Great Britain's Fir…/" I was cut off, for it spoke over me in its exquisite English accent … "I sir, am *The* Brompton, he/him/dog. Pleased to make your acquaintance *The* Bear!" I was impressed by The Brompton, he was clearly a well-educated beast, so I asked, "Did you go to Eaton? Or Oxbridge perchance?" To which he kicked back his head and pricked up an ear, "Oh no sir, I am from Mitch-E-Gan, United States of the USA!" So I said "But why the English accent *The* Brompton?"

We could have nattered all night, but this is a monologue which, by its very nature, rarely has allowance for two-character dialogue or duologues, so on with the story at hand!

We were just about to take a stroll, when, all of a terrible sudden, a dark, cloaked man stood high above us, he looked disheveled, disorientated, disbelieving, but worse of all, distasteful! This man spoke in a deep, sullen Scottish accent, "Izat yoo Bobby, ma wee lad?" He swooped down to grab a hold of my newfound friend and I knew I had to save The Brompton, so I flew up and lunged at this caped kidnapper of canines! My teeth, in full sparkling light bit into the cloaked codger's neck, but would you believe me when I say I flew straight through him? As if he was not there? No, I still do not understand this now! I landed on the wet grass and turned, only to see this man stroking my cheery chum, his tail wagged. The man spoke once more. "Yooo, laddy, are just like ma wee Bobby, let's go find 'im … ach! E's gotta be aboot 'ere somewhere! Follow me, 'n bring ya wee bear friend too!" We wondered around this chilling churchyard until the man stopped, held up his arms and proclaimed, "There he be, a shoulda noon! Wee Bobby 'as sat by me grave for fourteen years since the day I passed, bless 'is wee soul!" My Bear fur stood on end, The Brompton bowed his head and wagged his tail, for before us sat the ghost of a tired old terrier, this old man's Bobby. Not another word was spoke, The Brompton took a few paces forward and stood nose to nose with Bobby, together they politely nodded, looked up to the moon and let out little howls in unison, to which I admit, I let out a little tear. Then the man appeared over Bobby, clipped a leash to his collar before walking off into the night, disappearing before our disbelieving eyes.

I looked to The Brompton, he looked to The Bear, then he said "Gosh, look at the time, I really should check in on Jacquie and Jeff, heaven knows what mischief they will be getting up to! Hop on my back, let's head back!" Soon enough we were insight of our people, his folks called out "BROMPTON!", Jonathan called out "BEAR!" Re . . . U . . . Nighted!

There followed an evening of joy, of beer, of whiskey and stories of old in a public house called 'The Greyfriars Bobby'. Jonathan's family had met new friends, while Brompton and I raised a dog bowl to Bobby, a fine fellow if ever there was. Someone should make a statue of him!

<u>PART 9 - BEARS ON A PLANE!</u>

In this sky-high adventure, we join Bear on a flight to New York, most of the journey has passed without noticeable event, until the plane they are in gets caught up in a terrible thunderstorm, which brings to life all stuffed animals on board.

BEAR: This is the story of how I, Great Britain's First Ever Vampire Teddy Bear, foiled . . . no . . . this time find out for yourselves, no spoilers here!

Twas a dark and stormy flight, yes your ears heard correctly, a dark and stormy flight. We were flying in one of those great big white metal tube things the humans call an aerocraft. Jonathan had won a trip to New York, which included free entry to the third annual Stuffed Toy Animal Convention in Queens, so naturally I was brought along. As a result, there were many types of bears and other stuffed toy animals sharing our journey, each cradled in their little humans' arms. One such Bear I took an immediate disliking to, he had a shabby coat, torn ear, one plastic eye and his stitching was coming undone. Understandable for a wizened old bear as I'm sure you'll agree, however something seemed amiss about this one, was it his all-seeing eye, was it the way he grimaced, who can tell? I chose to keep my eyes on this possible perpetrator of planes. I sat back and relished a return trip to the Big Apple, so that I could continue my rudely interrupted takeover of Manhattan!

We were high above the Atlantic Sea when the pilot

warned us all, in his funny nasally voice, that there may well be a storm ahead. This did not worry Jonathan one iota, for he was concentrating on his cartoon film, cleverly being played out on a little screen in the back of the seat afore us. We had already been on this flight for some hours, Jonathan's father was sleeping, snoring and slobbering while his mother watched a movie on her own screen, something about there being many shades of the colour grey. Whatever it was, she was very . . . engrossed. I took this opportunity to converse with another teddy across the aisle, between watching the lovely legs of our flight attendant Melissa, as she paced up and down the narrow corridor, her slender legs in shiny black high heels, stockings, short skirt . . . ahem, sorry, where was I? Ah yes, the other Ted, who introduced himself as Tedward Van Helsing, proclaiming himself as Germany's first ever Vampire Teddy Bear . . . hahaha would you believe that! He was a fine fellow, dark black in fur, excellent stitching, well stuffed with fine marble eyes. We discussed many ongoing political issues around the world as well as joking about just how many picnics Yogi managed to steal.

With barely an hour remaining of our flight the aerocraft began to shake, little lights came on above all our heads and Melissa told us all to buckle up and remain calm. Jonathan dropped me on the floor, the careless mite, but thankfully Melissa picked me up, gave me a lovely little cuddle before placing me back in his arms. Oh, she smelled so sweet! Pretty soon after, the aerocraft began to shake some more, great flashes of lightning belted past either side of the little round windows. Then, all of a terrible sudden, one lightning bolt must have struck this great metal beast, for there was an almighty crash-bang! Jonathan cried out and looked to his mother, who held him tight but remained fixated to her movie, while his father's head rose, mumbled something incoherent, then slumped and snored some more. Our kindly captain told us that there was nothing to worry about, and that we'd soon be making our decent into New York. But all was far from well . . .

To be continued . . .

Now!

But all was far from well. For gradually, one by one, all the stuffed toys on this flight came alive, yes, I swear it! Clearly Tedward Van Helsing and myself have always been very much alive, immortal even, but it is highly unlikely that other bears and likewise stuffed animal variations will take on human-like life. But on this flight they did and they all ran amok! Oh the calamity! Black and white badgers, floppy eared blue bunnies, orange orangutangs, mauve monkeys, hairy hounds, colourful cats, peppered pigs and anything else you care to rhyme were all shouting, singing and jumping from seat to seat! This was quite a bizarre sight so Van Helsing and I tutted our disapproval and tried to pick up our discussion on the invasion of Ukraine and what this would mean to Martha and her family. But events from went bad to worse . . . plates, glasses, handbags, shoes, life jackets etcetera etcetera, were now being thrown here-all-over by this unruly rabble! Poor Melissa was doing her best to grab any plush toy she could and reunite them with their kiddy owners, but still they leapt about in their ridiculous rambunctiousness. She looked to us both as if to say, "Why aren't you two affected?" So Van Hesling looked to me, I looked to Van Helsing and in that moment we knew we simply had to intervene. After one quick nod we jumped into action, we charged, we flew, we caught, we sunk our bear fangs into, and we downed them one by one until each and every stuffed animal had been floored, pinned down by their humans.

We were about to take our seats with our human friends when I noticed that the scruffy one-eyed bear was no-bear to be seen. I asked my German pal if he'd seen him but he simply shook his head . . . I had to find this dastardly demon bear! Then Jonathan shouted out, "It's up there!" Van Helsing and I looked up to see the threadbare bear running along the roof, up-side-down! Not only was he incredibly apt at this tantalising task, he was pulling and ripping at the overhead baggage compartments. Too soon was he inside one and what ensued was a barrage of flying bags, laptops, hats, scarfs, berets . . . but worst of all, yes far worse . . . aerocraft wires! This badly groomed bum was ripping the whole place apart! Van Helsing leapt up in a rage but was swiped clear by a Prada handbag. Oh the indignity! I helped him to his feet and we hatched a plan to distract this mangy monster.

As planned, Van Helsing rushed up the aisle to find Melissa and in seconds they returned together, Melissa had a bottle of pepper spray in her hand which she proceeded to fire in the direction of the rascally ruffian. On her third spray she got him right in his eye! Way to go Melissa! Van Helsing flew up and knocked him to the floor of the aisle where I lay in wait, bear fangs glistening! Moments later the beaten bear was laying sedated at my paws. All the passengers were cheering "Bear!" "Bär!" "Bears!"

Melissa was so impressed by our heroics she took us to meet the Captain, what an honour! We made our way up to the front, each of us in the soft arms of this gorgeous air stewardess. Once in the cockpit we realised the full extent of the terrible storm. Melissa cried out, "What's going on Captain Sully?" to which he explained that Co-Pilot Johnson had been knocked unconscious from when the plane had been struck by lightning. As if that wasn't bad enough the starboard engine had failed due to wires being ripped out of the cabin! We did not have enough power to get to the airport, but Captain Sully thought quickly and insisted that his only remaining option was to land in the Hudson River!

Melissa spoke next, "Bears, you help the Captain while I calm the passengers!" And she was gone! Van Helsing radioed the control tower while I jumped onto the lap of the sleeping Co-Pilot. Captain Sully shouted out his orders to me and I did my beary best to help while he wrestled with the controls. Slowly and shakily, we descended until we could see the tall towers of New York either side of us.

A few scary moments later the competent captain had safely landed us on the river! Melissa and her colleagues were guiding the thankful passengers off the aerocraft and onto the wings and inflated rafts to await rescue from the good people of New York. Captain Sully, who I must say sounded just like Woody from the movie Toy Story, reunited us with our humans and we too were taken to safety. Even Jonathan's father had woken during the bumpy watery landing!

A week after this tumultuous event, Both Tedward Van Helsing and I, along with our respective families, Melissa and Captain Sully, were guests of honour at the third annual Stuffed Toy Animal Convention in Queens! All in a day's work for Great Britain's first ever Vampire Teddy Bear!

PART 10 - THE BEAR WITH THE GOLDEN FUR!

In this grand finale, Bear embarks on his most epic adventure yet. He is hired by MI5 to help them infiltrate a criminal mastermind, a Bear of Gold.

BEAR: This is the story of how I, Great Britain's first ever Vampire Teddy Bear, took on the most dangerous criminal bear-mind in the whole big world!

Twas a dark and stormy night, Jonathan had me on his lap in the back seat of the family's motorcar as we drove, splashing through the soggy streets of London. Lightning flickered high over Big Ben making its subtle reflection shimmer off the River Thames. We were returning from hospital where the little mite's father had had a scare, a murmur in his heart, but the dashing Dr Noh said he was lucky and there was "Noh-thing" to worry about. Please! I spent the journey reading and re-reading the postcard I had received the day before from the marvelous Melissa, the beautiful air stewardess from my escapade in the air.

It read:

"To my Dearest Bear, this week I write to you from Moscow, it's rather chilly and I wish you were here to keep me warm with your soft plush fur! Until we meet again my sweet Bear, from Russia with Love, Melissa (kiss kiss, bang bang!)"

I read it once more for luck before carefully putting it in my satchel with the other fourteen postcards from my new love. I was pleased she managed to visit Moscow because she always wanted to see the Gremlin, to which she laughed that gorgeous giggle at me when I suggested she just watch the film. I will never truly understand human women.

We passed by the front gates of Buckingham Palace and marveled at the Victoria Memorial Statue, gallantly pointing her gold finger to the heavy clouds above. A great thunder ball of lightning crashed down on Pall Mall behind us making Jonathan jump in his seat. We were lucky we were not struck, for you humans, unlike immortal bears such as myself, you only live twice! Jonathan's father had to stop the car suddenly along with a barrage of expletives I do not care to repeat, for a big black motorcar had stopped right in our path! Two dark figures emerged from said motorcar, paced up to us and one knocked heavily on the side window. The window was wound down to a tall shadow of a man who leaned in and said, "Official business sir, we need The Bear." Jonathan's parents protested until the other dark figure opened the door, a lady this time, equally dressed all in black but her voice was kind and soft, "Do excuse us, may we borrow The Bear? You see, he is needed on Her Majesties' Secret Service" She gave a subtle smile and in that very instance I recognised her. Heather! You remember, from when we thwarted those ne'er-do-wells in the Millenium Dome? She leant in, plucked me from Jonathan's lap and with a little kiss on my forehead, we were off!

There followed a journey of haste through London, I in the arms of Heather while I questioned just what on Earth was happening. I explained that while it was obviously very pleasing to see my marvelous millennium miss, it was rather unsettling for my family of humans to see me whisked away in such a fashion. She simply gave a small, sympathetic smile and told me all will become clear soon, "Relax Dear Bear." In a matter of a few short minutes, we arrived at a strange, grey, stepped building overlooking the River Thames. To some, this gloomy building could seem intimidating, but to a vampire bear with a live and let die attitude it did not phase me at all. After passing through what seemed like endless rounds of tight security measures, we arrived at an office door with the letter M on it. Sat at a desk by this door was a secretary, a rather stunning secretary at that, who introduced herself as Miss Spend-a-Penny. I flashed her my best flirtatious smile to which she rolled her eyes and told me to go through the door, M was waiting. Inside, Heather and I stood facing a large mahogany table and behind that a tall black leather chair swiveled its back toward us. Heather coughed politely . . . nothing, so she coughed a little less politely until the chair turned round. Sat in the chair was none other than Dame Judy Dench herself! Ha, would you believe it? Dame Judy looked stern, stoic and serious, her arms folded tight as she addressed us, "Ah, Bear, so glad you can join us. I'm sorry for your somewhat unorthodox abduction, but this is serious." However, I was distracted, confused, even bemused. "But are you not an actress, who played M in those films on the televisual box my humans watch?" To which she replied, "I can see your confusion Bear, being an actor is simply cover, for really I am the head of MI6. Playing the part of M, was, I dare say, a little ironic!" She gave a sweet chuckle before turning deadly serious once more. "Bear, we need your help, we need to infiltrate the Bureau of Evil Awful Ruffians, better known as B.E.A.R.S. This is where you come in, we need you to remove its leader, a formidable character known to the Bureau as The Bear With The Golden Fur. Heather will fill you in." Dame Judy swiveled back around in her chair to which we took as our dismissal. Outside M's door I expertly threw my satchel across the room and watched as it caught on a hook just below a black hat. Miss Spend-A-Penny was clearly impressed. "James Bond, the spy who loved me, had such similar skills, that was his hat. Welcome aboard…. Double-0-Seven!"

… the name's Bear, *The* Bear. let me take you to double oh heaven!

Heather tutted, grabbed my arm and we were off, we had to put a stop to this evil, awful ruffian of a bear! We soon found ourselves in a rather swish private aerocraft called The Moonraker, heading for an undisclosed Middle Eastern country, where Heather was able to fill me in on the criminal corporation called B.E.A.R.S. Champagne in hand she explained all about these ruffians, and her position as Double-O-Six within MI6. We had time to relax so I told her about my many adventures as Great Britain's first ever Vampire Teddy Bear. Heather soon grew tired, and headed for her private chamber, so I looked out across the wing at the setting sun, wondering just what further adventures may lay ahead. Moments later her chamber door opened, her long slender arm, clad only in the finest, thinnest silk, beckoned me to her. Naturally I picked up the bottle of Dom Bearignon, followed in an instant, as she closed the door behind us, she seductively said "For your eyes only … Bear"

Two days later we took our table in a Japanese restaurant in the capital city of UMEC (Undisclosed Middle Eastern Country.) While we were tucking into some strange rice coated seafood dishes, Heather explained that the fish with eight legs was "Octopus, see." But I was otherwise distracted, for there on a shelf high above the service desk was a teddy bear. Not just any bear, this bear was scruffy and old, with a wispy beard and odd, glassy green eyes which seemed to be scanning round the room. Heather soon picked up on my unease, asked if I was alright, but when we looked up the bear was not there! Were my bear eyes deceiving me, could I not bear to believe that the bear I saw there was barely even there? Where was this bear? I put it down to the unusually uncooked fish making me hallucinate, I will never eat such rice clad fishy dishes again! I know 'never say never!' Again, this scruffy bear appeared, this time right in my face brandishing a sharp pointed knife! I ducked as Heather cried out, the aged ted was fast for an old bear, he swished the knife around my head nigh on taking my ears off! But this old bear was no match for Great Britain's first ever Vampire Teddy Bear, as I ducked and dived, froze and flew, I took my opportunity to nod to Heather. My sexy sidekick stabbed the battered bear with a chopstick knocking him to the table as I sank my bear fangs into his dusty neck! It was clear to us we had had our first encounter with a member of B.E.A.R.S.

Early next morning Heather and I parted company, she to interrogate the wispy old bear in the restaurant to see if he had connections, while I began to hunt down the famous golden furred ruffian. Miss Spend-A-Penny had given me directions of where this bear was thought to have his lair. Once nearby I decided it was best to stake out the joint, so I took position in a minaret which looked down over Bears-R-Us toy shop. How clever to blend into his surroundings, this bear was smarter than the average bear! I watched as bears, some innocently going about their business, some looking shady, visited the shop, it's little overdoor bell signaling each one's arrival. I waited patiently for their leader to immerge, knowing I could swoop down on him taking him by complete surprise and sinking two long teeth into his sorry neck, it was the perfect view to a kill. But time passed, I grew hungry so thought it best to join Heather back at the Japanese restaurant. Barely minutes from said eatery a tuktuk flashed by scaring the living daylights out of me! I was shaken, but not stirred. This rattly old colourful machine screeched to a halt and out popped an air hostess! "Bear!" she called, asking if it was really me. Yes . . . you've guessed it, Melissa, standing there in flesh and blood, I in stuffing and fur. We jumped together into the tuktuk and headed to a bar Melissa knew well from her travels. Here we drank vodka martinis as she explained why she found herself in the capital city of UMEC. Her aerocraft had been diverted from Bahrain due to rather too many snakes on it, which had given the pilot the shakes, so now Melissa had time to kill. I proclaimed, "You have time to kill, I have a License to kill!" so we laughed, we drank, we cuddled and we giggled, we drank more vodka until all become quite hazy, foggy, my stuffing mind full of fuzzy . . .

I awoke, with the heaviest head, under a big white dome which loomed over me, for I was on my back, strapped down onto a bench, oh the indignity! Fine paintings of glorious golden bears adorned the curves of this beautiful vast vault. So how the blazers did I get here? Only moments ago I was enjoying amorous air hostess attention, now I'm restrained in some sort of elaborate bear lair?

Then, all of a terrible sudden, the bench I was restrained on tilted up so I could see directly ahead of me a huge giant of a bear! He must have stood six feet tall, taller than Jonathan's father even, bigger than any bear I had ever laid my bear eyes on. His fur, yes you've guessed, was as gold as gold can be, even from a distance this was a superior build bear if ever there was. His stuffing bulged like muscles, even his stitching was of fine filigree gold. How annoyingly perfect was this bear? I called out "Found you!" to which this brightly coated giant of a bear simply shook his head and walked towards me. Up close I could see just how exquisite this ted really was, except one strange thing . . . he only had one golden eye, the other was a camera! Now that IS clever! He waved his gold paw in the air to which a slender, slinky, sleek and sexy lady sashayed up to the golden bear. She herself dressed in the tightest sparkly gold bodysuit, her legs in golden boots, gold lace gloves on her hands, but when I finally looked up to see her face, I was aghast! "Melissa?" Is no-one in this story really who they make out to be?

"Oh Bear," she said "It was oh so easy! A kiss on your head, a cuddle, a couple of vodkas, now look at you, mwah hahaha" At this point she kicked her head back with her attempt at an evil laugh, her long dark curly hair flowing over her perfect glistening gold shoulders …concentrate Bear! This was no time for furry fuzzy feelings, my life was on the line. I was tilted back to once again look up into this sensational ceiling, until suddenly the mosaics and murals vanished to be replaced by thousands of screens. On each screen a scene began to unfold, all of them films of bears, teddy bears of all shapes, sizes, colours and build quality. They had one thing in common, they all had one camera eye, the other gold.

The Bear with the Golden Fur began to speak, in a deep indecipherable eastern European accent, "Hmm, Gweat Brittens Virst ever Vampire Teddy Vear, ve meet at larst . . ." He laughed once, the delicious dirty double-crossing Melissa laughed too. He went on, "Each an' every bear haz ze camera as an eye you see, with ze vision zay give me I can control ze vorld. You might ask vhat is ze other eye? It iz ze lazer!" It took me a while to decide which was most appalling, his plan for world domination or his disdainful accent! Either way the gilded bear had to be stopped! I struggled against the restraints with all my might but could not break free, so it was my turn to speak, "You'll never get away with this! I am immortal, for me tomorrow never dies!" The big bullion brute of a bear turned away laughing, with Melissa following as they disappeared through the door.

I was left alone, staring up into the dome. The scenes on the screens were all quite similar, bears and their human children, going about their daily routine, but something was odd . . . I studied each and every one, then a pattern emerged, every bear was slowly taking control of their child friend! Think Bear, think! Just as I was going batty with despair, it occurred to me! A bat! Turn into a bat, Bear! I clenched my eyes, concentrated hard, I dreamed, I fantasised about flying in the dome. When I opened my eyes I was really flying, I looked to my arms to see they had miraculously transformed into bat wings! Well I never, I can do the bat thing after all! I flew around the room looking for a way out, when finally I found an air vent just big enough to squeeze through. Once inside I resumed bear status and scurried along lengths and lengths of ducting until I heard a voice, or rather an annoyingly awful accent. The Bear with the Golden Fur was right below me, standing over a desk with lots of controls surrounding one big gold button. Nearby I found another vent which I was able to pull inside, providing enough room for a clever little bat. I flew out, swooped and swiped around his head. He shouted lots of bizarre expletives and I very nearly had this rascally bear, but one big swipe from his golden paw and I was floored! I stood back up in Bear form and flashed my sharp white bear fangs.

"You var too late Mister Bear, it az begun, bearz around ze vorld are taking over! And once zay have I will also concur ze planet Mars, for ze vorld iz not enough!" This was one deranged ruffian bear! Then, all of a terrible sudden he pulled out a golden gun and shot at me! How dare he! The bullet passed clean through me, you should have seen the look of shock on his face so I told him, "I am immortal remember, whereas you, if not this instance, will die another day!" At that I leapt up onto the control desk, activated the emergency stop and jumped for this golden bears neck. My bear fangs dug deep through his fur right into his stuffing, he staggered some before crashing to the ground! Paralyzed at my feet I jumped back onto the console only to see I had accidently triggered the self-destruct button! Whoops! I had to get out fast, I scurried for the door to the dome room, charged though it only to be halted by the most unexpected sight, Golden Girl Melissa fighting with my sexy sidekick Heather! As tempting as it was to find some popcorn and sit back to watch, we still had to escape, so I called out, "Melissa, I love you!" Melissa stopped fighting, turned to face me, which gave Heather just enough time knock her down with one big kick!

There was no time to stare, the building was beginning to collapse around us, so we were off! We found another door out of the big white room which lead outside to a small yard, where a golden bear-mobile was parked, Heather shouted for me to get in and she drove us away with much haste. As she sped from this evil bear lair, I looked back to see it crumble to the ground, with only the front door of the shop remaining with the sign reading Bears-R-Us.

I suggested we celebrate our victory with a bottle of Dom Bearignon at the Casino Royale, but Heather was not so happy, she explained that she was upset because

I said to Melissa that I love her. Honestly, you human women! It was a ruse and it worked. But Heather needed some time out, some space, a quantum of solace, whatever she meant about that I will never know. I spent the evening alone in the bar where I had drunk with Melissa. Heather was now my love, my one true love, I had bared my heart to her, now it seemed she wanted nothing more to do with this humble bear. I thought I would see my world implode, my sky fall.

Heather and I flew on the same aerocraft home, sat across the aisle, not speaking. She looked pale, sad, ghostly, like a spectre. I leaned back to close my eyes when a familiar voice spoke to me, "Glass of champagne Mr Bear?" I looked up to see Melissa, in full air hostess attire! She thanked me for all what I had done and for releasing her from The Bear with the Golden Fur's evil awful spell. I turned to see Heather giving me daggers, not literally, the looks I mean. Then she laughed out loud, kicking her head back in her hysterics, "I'm teasing you Bear, can't you see that?"

A few hours later the aerocraft touched down back in England, the stairs were lowered and I prepared myself for the inevitable adulation from my fans. Instead, on the tarmac was Dame Judy M, standing alone by a long black motorcar. "Bear, you must come with me to the hospital, your family need you." Jonathan? Is it my best friend Jonathan? What has happened to my best friend? His father? He has a murmur! So many questions raced through my mind as we sped to the hospital. Dame Judy rushed me in herself and in no time we were in a private room where figures huddled round a bed. One figure was Jonathan, who turned to see me first and called out, "BEAR!" then his mother looked to me, followed by his father. I was confused, Jonathan's parents were clearly upset but they were all well. His mother lifted me up and placed me by a sweet old lady laying in the bed. The poor old dear turned her head very slowly to me, her tired grey eyelids opened just slightly. As she saw me her eyes opened wide in wonderment, she coughed gently then just managed to say, "Is that really you? Bear?" Her voice was oddly familiar and when I looked close, I could see that same mischievous twinkle in her eyes . . . "Hilda?" She smiled and held me in close, I could smell her perfume and memories of our time in the old wooden chalet in Switzerland came flooding back.

She spoke once more, "Jonathan, this is a very special bear, you must always cherish him." To which he replied, "Of course I will Grandma." Hilda snuggled me tight to her chest and I could hear her heart beat slower and slower.

For the first time in my long life, I shed some real tears. I whispered to her, "Hilda, be strong, just like you were in Frankfurt, this is no time to die."

END OF PLAY

<u>EPILOGUE</u>
<u>PART 11 - BATTY IN BEARMUDA</u>

Bear has been enjoying a well-earned extended vacation in Bearmuda, a time to rest his weary mind and body after his many escapades. But there is a dark force afoot on these tropical Islands, so jumps back to action.

BEAR: This is the story of how I, Great Britain's first ever Vampire Teddy Bear saved the British Colonial Islands of Bearmuda from a batty demise!

Twas a bright and sunny day, like many were during my extended sabbatical following many tiring escapades. I was taking tea at Government House, guest of honour invited by the Governor of Bearmuda, Rena Gallie. Sat sitting on some green rattan chairs, the fine Italianate façade of Government house behind us, we discussed world politics, the state of the financial crisis in Uzbekistan, the Bearmuda Triangle and Dark 'N Stormy Rum. Rena described just how this rum came to be the island nation's national drink, devised by merchant sailors and named after the sensational sea storms said sailors survived. As we sat back and admired the view of many wonderous yachts floating serenely in The Sound, the sea gently lapping at their bows, a lady servant of the governor, introduced as Blessing, came up to us, bowed politely and gave Rena a newspaper.

Once Blessing had collected up the fine bone China cups, saucers and ornate teapot, Rena laid out the days copy of the Bearmudan Times on the little table between us. 'Tut tut tut' she said. I enquired into the reason of her mild distaste at the headline, so she held aloft the front page for me to see. It read: 'Vampire Bats of Bearmuda Bite Again!' Oh dear, dear, oh dear! It turns out many residents and tourists visiting these wonderful tropical islands had succumbed to a rather unwelcome plague of Vampire Bats! Some poor souls even found themselves in the hospital, other less fortunate folks ended up in the asylum where they would try to climb the walls at night or would attempt to fly out of the windows.

So naturally, being Great Britain's first ever Vampire Teddy Bear, I offered my services to Rena and the good people of Bearmuda. At haste she organised a speedy boat to take me, and Blessing as my guide, to the north-easternmost peninsula to a place where these rascally winged rodents reside, The Crystal Caves!

Pretty soon we found ourselves in these dark and mysterious caves late at night, waiting for the badly behaved bawdy bats to take flight. The tourists had all gone home, the lights had been lowered by the custodian of the caves and Blessing and I lay in wait. The subtle light reflected on crystal clean water and shimmered on the vast ceilings of this cool underground lair. Blessing described to me the stalagmites and stalactites which pointed up and down throughout, like vampire teeth in fact. She also explained a neat trick to remember which is which, 'Mites up, Tites down.' Oh I say!

Just as we grew tired and weary in the gentle sleepy light, we were awoken by strange and echoey flapping sounds, and all of a terrible sudden, thousands of big black brutal bats took flight! You should have seen the spectacle of this multi-arial display, almost a fog of flittering flying fiends, their tiny little vampire teeth sparkling in the light. Blessing was scared, I was astounded, and the bats were, well… being bats. I told her to fear not, Great Britain's first ever Vampire Teddy Bear was here! I stood up, concentrated on becoming a bat myself, with eyes closed tight, I took flight. Well, that was my intention, honestly, but what actually happened, as Blessing will no doubt recall, was me jumping, in Teddy Bear form, straight into the water! I was soaked! Blessing, bless her, quickly rescued me and helped dry me off, but my fur was drenched and my ego saturated, oh the indignity! After a good canine type shake which I learned from my doggy friend, The Brompton, I took to the dank cave air, this time as a vampire bat myself, probably Great Britain's first ever Vampire Bat haha! I flitted betwixt these flapping fellows as I tried to find their fearless leader before they flew to the freedom of the night. It was some arial feat, believe me, to fly in such numbers, so I was lucky to notice a bigger bat, with longer black wings whom the others followed. But all of a terrible sudden, Blessing cried out a shrill scream! I immediately swooped down to see what was up when I could see her grappling with a large bat at her neck! I flew onto the back of this blasted bat and sank my bear fangs into his own soft hairy neck, one quick bite and he was floored at Blessings feet. She smiled then quickly warned me as another bellowing bat bore down on me, so I jumped sideways, and he crashed into the water with an almighty splash!

As I regained my composure, I saw above us their lavish leader and soon I managed to join in behind this sergeant of blood suckers and flew in his slipstream. I called out to him to 'stop and hang with me for a while.' Naturally he was completely surprised to see a bat bear flying amongst his folks and even more astonished that I could speak fluent English. He agreed to meet me on the cave floor near to Blessing, as hanging upside down would make the stuffing go to my head. Once grounded, the other bats, by instinct, returned to the cave ceiling and tucked themselves back in their wings. Their leader introduced himself as Barry the Bat, Bearmuda's first ever Vampire Bat, well I never!

We spoke for a while as I expressed Rena's revulsion to having the necks of her people bitten in such ways by his rampaging rodent rascals, not to mention what effect it was having on Bearmuda's tourism. Barry flashed his big white fangs at me, and just as I thought he would attack, he simply apologised explaining that his kind always need blood. As I began to plead with Barry the Bat that there must be a solution to this dilemma a clever thought crossed my mind. So, I asked Barry if he had ever tried Bloody Mary cocktails, maybe they could substitute their insatiable need for blood? Barry seemed confused but also intrigued, Blessing looked simply befuddled as she rubbed her neck, so I suggested we meet on the lawn of The Governors house at dusk the following eve.

At dusk the following eve, Barry, Blessing and Rena met me on her lawn and Barry tried his first Bloody Mary Cocktail. He sipped, he grimaced, he shuddered, he flapped his wings, he burped… then he smiled, a big happy beaming smile, his fangs glistening in the moonlight. Then the next thing he did took us all by surprise, for he produced a torch, or flashlight as they say here, turned on the beam, held it under his wing and shone a great big bat wing signal into the sky, clever stuff! Within minutes a great cloud of his colony friends formed above our heads until they all swooped down to the ground.

The following sight was a sight to behold, let me tell you! Never before has any human or bear witnessed hundreds of bats standing on a lawn, sipping Virgin Mary Cocktails, chatting and dancing! For Rena had organised the island's steel drum band to play for us as Blessing and the other servants busily brewed these bats' new delicious cocktail in one big cauldron of a pot.

I took up the mic to sing:

"Now all you bats are here,

You'll find there's no more fear,

Try to see it from Bears angle,

The Bearmuda Triangle,

It's not so bad!"

As the night drew on and the party began to draw to a close, one by one the tired, slightly drunken bats flew back to their caves, Rena took me to one side. "Bear" she said, "There's someone I think you should meet." An hour later we found ourselves in the Bearmuda asylum, a dark and dank establishment full of sad and sorry souls. Rena guided Blessing and I to a top story floor, she opened a big steel door and there, curled up in the corner was a quivering, jabbering, lightly bearded New Yorker. Rena explained that he was their asylum's first resident to have two bite marks on his neck and that he calls himself 'Renfield' but his real name was Scott. As if he sensed us, he spun round in a second, stood up at a stoop and shouted out in a croaky cry, "MASTER!" I immediately recognised this call, for it has haunted my dreams for many years. Rena asked if there was anything to be done for this poor man, to which I pondered, for I was weak and weary from the busy day. Then the perfect idea popped into the stuffing of my mind. My dear Renfield, I said, you may serve your master by taking up a position in the Crystal Caves . . . as Chief Bat Caretaker! He cried out "YES MASTER!"

Back at The Governors house, Rena bid us good night, for she had other business to attend to the following morning. And as Blessing and I took a moment to gaze across The Sound, she looked up in the sky and opened her mouth to reveal two great big white fangs which sparkled in the moonlight! Then she cried out, "I AM BLESSING, BOW BENEATH MY FEET AND TREMBLE, FOR I AM BEARMUDAS FIRST EVER VAMPIRE HUMAN, MWAH HA HA HA HA!!"

THE END.

...FOR NOW.

57

NOTES

(Use this space to make notes for your production)

58

BOBBY IS DEAD

by Marty Matfess

2M, 3W, COMEDY

Chris has been madly in love with his best friend Annie for years, but she's only been interested in dating everyone else but him. After Annie's recent break up with her boyfriend Bobby, Chris feels this may finally be what he needs to find his way into her heart, but just like that ... she's already moved on to another guy she met at a coffee shop. Being the good friend that he is, Chris has agreed to hang out with the new guy's visiting sister while they go out on a date. Oh, and let's not forget about Bobby. Turns out he's not taking the breakup too well and Chris is now caught between an aggressive ex-boyfriend while having to keep new guy's sister company. A play about love, lust, and getting shot in the head.

IN THE SLUSH

by Daniel Prillaman

2M, 2W, HORROR, DRAMA

2023 FINALIST FOR NEW DRAMATISTS' PRINCESS GRACE AWARD

Newlywed Laura Beth Gardner has it all. A loving husband, a baby on the way, and a usually delightful job. But this weekend, tasked with reading through her publishing house's slush pile, she encounters a mysterious manuscript that claims she isn't human. That her husband isn't who he says he is. And that she's a vessel for her unborn child, who is actually the Second Coming of an ancient darkness that will devour the world. It has to be some sort of joke.

…But what if it's not?

A cosmic horror about identity, creation, and the things we'll do to realize our dreams.